S0-BEI-648

CORDUROY'S HALLOWEEN

BASED ON THE CHARACTER BY DON FREEMAN

STORY BY B. G. HENNESSY

PICTURES BY LISA McCUE

SCHOLASTIC INC.

NEW YORK TORONTO LONDON AUCKLAND SYDNEY

It's fall! The air is colder, and the trees are turning red and yellow. Corduroy and his friends are having fun raking leaves into big piles. It is time to get ready for one of Corduroy's favorite holidays—HALLOWEEN!

First, Corduroy visits the pumpkin patch.
Picking the right pumpkin is hard work!
Should he pick a tall, skinny one or a round, fat one?

Next, Corduroy goes to the store. He buys black and orange paper, candles for the jack-o'-lantern, paints for the window-painting contest, treats for the trick-or-treaters, and everything he needs for his costume.

Today is the window-painting contest.
Everyone works very hard painting ghosts, monsters,
witches, cats, and bats. Corduroy paints a big, orange
pumpkin. Nice job, Corduroy!

Finally, it is Halloween.
Corduroy has put up his decorations.
He has carved two pumpkins—

one is scary, and one is silly. Even the treats are ready.
Knock, knock! The first trick-or-treaters are here!

"Trick-or-treat for *Unicef*!"

Now Corduroy is in his costume, and he joins the Halloween parade. Look at the ghosts, monsters, witches, animals, pirates, princesses, and pumpkins! Can you guess which one is Corduroy?

It's time for the Halloween party. It is Corduroy's turn to bob for apples. There are doughnuts and cider for everyone.

HAPPY HALLOWEEN!

DON FREEMAN was born in San Diego, California, and moved to New York City to study art, making his living as a jazz trumpeter. Following the loss of his trumpet on a subway train, Mr. Freeman turned his talents to art full-time. In the 1940s, he began writing and illustrating children's books. His many popular titles include *Corduroy*, *A Pocket for Corduroy*, *Beady Bear*, *Dandelion*, *Mop Top*, and *Norman the Doorman*.

LISA McCUE was born in Tappan, New York, and has illustrated more than seventy-five books, including *Corduroy's Christmas*, *Corduroy's Toys*, *Corduroy's Day*, and *Corduroy on the Go*. She lives in Bethlehem, Pennsylvania, with her husband and their two sons.

ISBN 0-590-74516-6

Text copyright © 1995 by Penguin Books USA Inc.
Illustrations copyright © 1995 by Lisa McCue.
All rights reserved. Published by Scholastic Inc., 555 Broadway, New York, NY 10012, by arrangement with Penguin Books USA Inc.

12 11 10 9 8 7 6 5 4 3   8 9/9 0 1/0

Printed in Malaysia   46

First Scholastic printing, September 1996